D0008339

13/10

THE CROOKED BOY

ISBN 0-89868-493-5–Library Bound
ISBN 0-89868-494-3–Soft Bound
ISBN 0-89868-495-1-Trade

A PREDICTABLE WORD BOOK

THE
CROOKED BOY

Story by Janie Spaht Gill, Ph.D.
Illustrations by Gerald Rogers

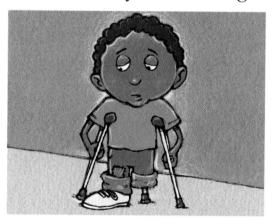

✳ ARO PUBLISHING

There was a crooked boy,
who looked like this.

He didn't like his crooked shape, or his crookedness.

He wandered down a crooked
road toward a crooked man.

He thought, "how much we are alike,
I know he'll understand.

10

Can you help me mister?
I don't like my crookedness."

"Indeed I can, my boy,"
the crooked man expressed.

"Crooked things are special,
they're different than the rest.

Because they're so unique,
some think crooked things are best.

The sandy shoreline is crooked
to carry the crooked sea.

16

There live the crab and seahorse,
both crooked as can be.

Bending trees are crooked
to fit their crooked limbs.

Jagged leaves are crooked
to fit their crooked stems."

"I see what you are saying," said the boy. "I'm no different than the rest.

21

Crooked things are all around us,
in fact crooked things are best."